The Passover
COWBOY

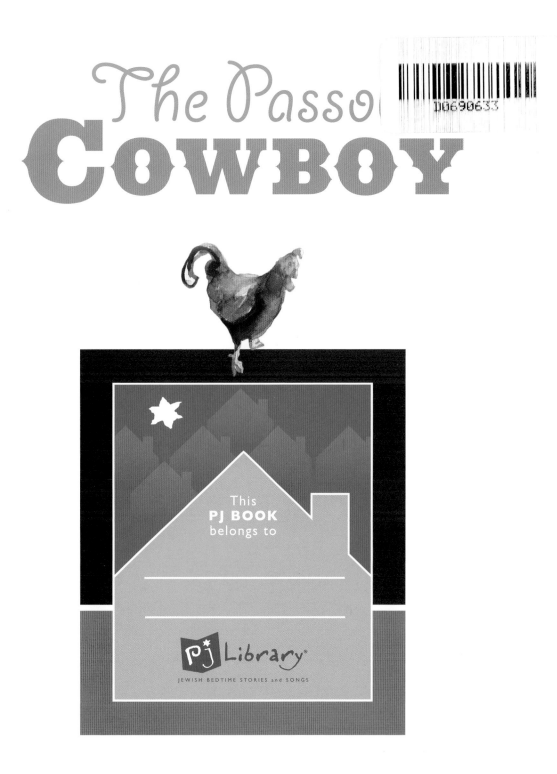

This
PJ BOOK
belongs to

_____

_____

PJ Library®

JEWISH BEDTIME STORIES and SONGS

By **Barbara Diamond Goldin**

Illustrated by **Gina Capaldi**

APPLES & HONEY PRESS

Springfield, NJ • Jerusalem

Dedicated to my granddaughter,
Hanna Sylvia, who loves horses and
most animals unless they're scary.
—BDG

To my mother, who encouraged
me to love all things historical.
—GC

Apples & Honey Press
An imprint of Behrman House and Gefen Publishing House
Behrman House, 11 Edison Place, Springfield, New Jersey 07081
Gefen Publishing House Ltd., 6 Hatzvi Street, Jerusalem 94386, Israel
www.applesandhoneypress.com

Text copyright © 2017 by Barbara Diamond Goldin
Illustrations copyright © 2017 by Gina Capaldi

ISBN 978-1-68115-527-2

Library of Congress Cataloging-in-Publication Data
Names: Goldin, Barbara Diamond, author. | Capaldi, Gina, illustrator.
Title: The Passover cowboy / by Barbara Diamond Goldin ; illustrated by
Gina Capaldi.
Description: Springfield, NJ : Apples & Honey Press, [2017] | Ages 4-8, K
to grade 3. | Includes bibliographical references and index.
Identifiers: LCCN 2016012114 | ISBN 9781681155272 (alk. paper)
Subjects: | CYAC: Passover—Juvenile fiction. | Seder—Juvenile fiction.
Classification: LCC PZ7.G5674 Pas 2016 | DDC [Fic]—dc23
LC record available at http://lccn.loc.gov/2016012114

Design by Elynn Cohen
Edited by Ann Koffsky and Dena Neusner
Made in China
9 8 7 6 5 4 3 2 1

031717K1/B0972/A7

Jacob and his cowboy friend, Benito, raced to the far fence post, Benito on his strong gray horse and Jacob on his pony, Rosa. Jacob had never gone so fast. And he hadn't fallen off once.

"You're almost ready for the spring rodeo," Benito said when Jacob caught up to him. "But you'll need your own lasso."

"I know," said Jacob. "And I'll need loose clothes like yours, too. Not these tight pants from the Old Country."

Jacob looked at his new friend. Benito had grown up here in Argentina and learned to ride as soon as he could walk.

Jacob wondered. . .should he ask Benito? He took a deep breath. "Passover starts tonight, and we're having a seder. In Russia, my friends would come, and it was a lot of fun. Please come."

Benito hesitated. "I've never been to a seder."

Jacob rushed in. "We tell the story of how, long ago, the Jewish people escaped a mean Pharaoh and became a free people. And we eat a lot of yummy foods. Please, will you come?"

"I don't know," said Benito. "My father needs me tonight, to help with the horses and cows."

Jacob tried not to show his disappointment. "I'll save you a seat next to me," he said. "Maybe you'll finish your chores early." Jacob waved good-bye. He had to hurry now. It was getting late.

As Jacob rode, he thought about the lasso and clothes he needed for the rodeo. He thought of how he missed his friends in Russia. How they would run in and out of each other's houses, one house right next to the other. It was very different here where everything was so far apart.

"Faster, faster," Jacob urged
Rosa.

On the way he saw Papa finishing his work
in the cornfields. Papa wore the loose, wide
pants called *bombachas* under his long, black,
Russian coat. Mama hadn't had time to make
Jacob a pair yet.

"Papa!" Jacob called, "I asked Benito if he
could come to the seder."

"Good idea," Papa called back. "Then if a
stray calf walks in when we open the door for
the Prophet Elijah, Benito can lasso it!"

When Jacob got home, he took Rosa to her stall, then tried to sneak into the house. But his big sister, Miriam, caught him.

"You were out riding with Benito, weren't you?" she scolded.

"And you've been sucking on a lemon," said Jacob.

"Passover starts tonight! And all you can think about are horses and Benito."

"Just wait until you see me at my first rodeo."

"Shh," said Mama, coming into the kitchen carrying buckets of water from the well. "If we all work hard, we'll soon be ready. And then I have a surprise for you two."

Miriam and Jacob stopped bickering. Side by side with Mama, they chopped nuts and grated apples.

Soon the little house filled with the wonderful smells Jacob remembered from Passover in Russia: roasted chicken and potato puddings, carrot and raisin stew, and the sweet apple and nut mixture called *charoset.*

Jacob took a deep breath and thought of how much Benito would love these sweet smells, too. If only he could come.

While Miriam set the table, Jacob filled the silver seder plate. Less than a year ago, they had wrapped it in a blanket and carried it across the ocean on a big boat to this new land.

"Mama, we need another chair. In case Benito comes," Jacob said.

Mama smiled. "Inviting guests to the seder is a good thing to do—it's a mitzvah! And Benito and his father have been such a big help to us with the fields, cows, and chickens."

"Benito won't come," Miriam said, her hands on her hips. "Why should he care about us or our holiday?"

"He cares," said Jacob. "He'll come." But deep inside, Jacob wasn't sure.

"Well, if he does come," said Mama, "maybe that will help Jacob concentrate on Passover and not wish he were out riding on the plains!"

Mama bent down and pulled out a box. "Have you forgotten about the surprise? New clothes for the holiday. Let's see how they fit."

Soon Miriam was dancing across the floor in her new dress. Jacob opened his, and unfolded the wide *bombachas* and warm red poncho Mama had sewn for him. Perfect for the rodeo. If only Mama could make lassos, too!

He heard Miriam mumble, "He acts like Benito, and now he'll look like Benito."

Jacob pretended not to hear her. He pictured himself riding in his new clothes. How they would flap and crackle in the wind.

When Papa came in from the fields, he looked at Jacob and laughed. "Only here would a Jewish boy get clothes like these for Passover!"

Soon the family was
sitting around the seder
table. Jacob kept looking
at the empty chair next to
him, feeling empty inside.

He was thinking of Benito, but also of the happy, noisy seders with his grandparents, aunts, uncles, cousins, and friends.

Then Papa stood up, lifting the flat bread, the matzah.

"Look at this bread," Papa said in his commanding voice. "It is the bread of slavery that our ancestors ate in Egypt. All who are hungry, let them come and eat."

Just then, there were loud noises at the door.

Jacob looked up at Papa.

Papa winked. "Could it be Elijah, coming a little early?"

Jacob jumped up and started to open the door. Something flew right by his face. He stepped backward, falling into Papa. It was a chicken, and two more followed, squawking and screeching. One chicken landed on the seder table, splashing the matzah ball soup and spraying Miriam, who screamed. Mama wasn't fast enough to catch the Passover plate, and it spilled all over the floor.

"Don't worry. I'll catch them," said Benito from the doorway. He grabbed the chicken on the table.

Then he caught another one under the table and ran after the third.

Soon all three of them were in his arms.

Papa, Mama, Miriam, and Jacob piled up at the door, watching Benito put the chickens in the coop and shut the gate.

"Benito, you came!" shouted Jacob.

"Of course," said Benito. "You asked me to." He held up a beautiful new lasso. "Here. I've been working on it for weeks. I wanted to surprise you."

Jacob took the lasso carefully in his hands. "You made it for me? I can't believe it! And Mama made me *bombachas* and a poncho. Now I can ride in the rodeo!"

"I never thought you would come," said Miriam.

"I wanted to see what this celebration of freedom was all about," said Benito. "You know, we struggled for our freedom, too, here in Argentina."

"Okay, okay," said Mama. "Enough standing by the open door. Inside. Before every animal out there comes to the seder." And she shooed everyone into the house.

They worked together to clean up the spills and messes, and soon they were all seated around the table, with Benito in the chair next to Jacob.

"Now where were we?" said Papa.

"The Four Questions," answered Jacob happily. He proudly chanted the first part in Hebrew and then in Spanish, "Why is this night different from all other nights?"

"What a good question for tonight," said Papa laughing. "Because we're in a new country full of surprises."

"And it's not every night chickens come to dinner," said Miriam, smiling.

"And good friends, too," Jacob added, looking at Benito.

A Note for Families

In the late 1880s, with the help of financier and philanthropist Baron Maurice de Hirsch, groups of Russian Jews moved to Argentina in the hopes that there they would be free from the discrimination and poverty they experienced in eastern Europe. By 1925, about twenty-five thousand Jews lived in villages on the plains of Argentina.

The story of Jacob's family is set in Rajil, one of the Argentine colonies in which Jews settled. In Rajil, Jews would often hire a gaucho to be their herdsman. The gauchos of Argentina were much like the cowboys of the American West: excellent horsemen admired for their bravery and skill.

In *The Passover Cowboy*, Benito mentions the struggle that the people of Argentina faced to achieve their freedom. Argentina was once under the rule of Spain; the Argentine people fought for and declared independence from Spain in 1816.

The Jewish people have a holiday that celebrates their struggle for freedom: Passover. On Passover, they commemorate the Israelites' Exodus from ancient Egypt through a ceremony called a seder, which consists of songs, stories, blessings, rituals, and, of course, a festive meal. As part of the ritual, participants fill a glass of wine and open the door to welcome the Prophet Elijah, hoping he will bring times of peace to all.

Discuss with your family: What would it be like to move to a whole new country with a different language and customs?